I CAN READ STORIES

FEATHERY FURRY TALES

Judy Hindley
Illustrated by Toni Goffe

Kingfisher Books

Kingfisher Books, Grisewood & Dempsey Ltd,
Elsley House, 24-30 Great Titchfield Street,
London W1P 7AD

First published in 1993 by Kingfisher Books
2 4 6 8 10 9 7 5 3 1

The material in this edition
was previously published by Kingfisher Books in
My Own Story Book (1990)

Text copyright © Judy Hindley 1990, 1993
Illustrations copyright © Toni Goffe 1990, 1993
All rights reserved.

BRITISH LIBRARY
CATALOGUING IN PUBLICATION DATA
A catalogue record for this book
is available from the British Library

ISBN 1 85697 036 1
Printed and bound in Hong Kong

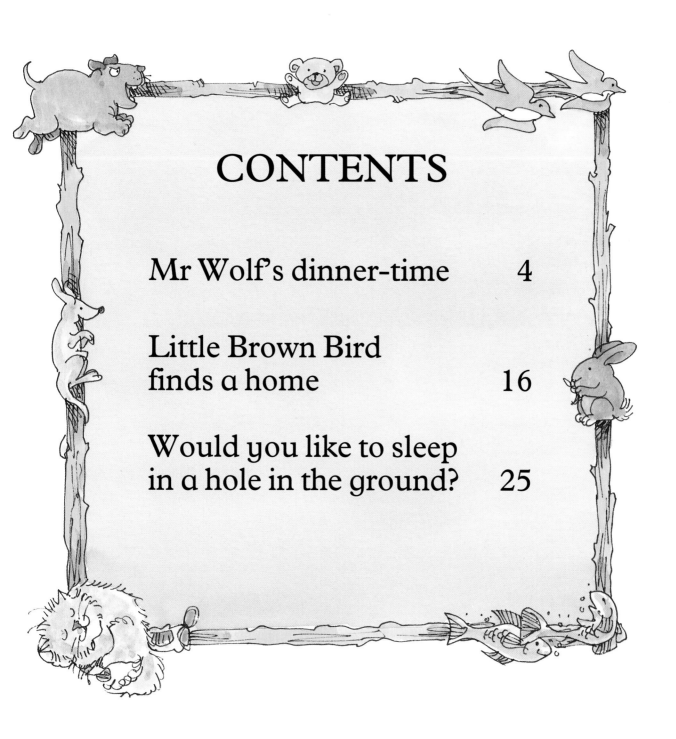

CONTENTS

Mr Wolf's dinner-time

A wolf
came to visit
some children.

He knocked
at the door.

KNOCK!
KNOCK!
KNOCK!

"Let me in," said the wolf.

"I am your mother, and it's time for dinner!"

"Oh, no!" cried the children. "You are not our mother. We can hear your sharp claws. Go away!"

The wolf
went away,
and clipped off
his sharp claws.

Then
he went back.

6

KNOCK!
KNOCK!
KNOCK!

"Let me in,"
said the wolf.
"I am
your mother,
and it's time
for dinner!"

"Oh, no!"
cried the children.
"You are not
our mother.
We can see
your sharp teeth.
Go away!"

The wolf
went away,
and filed down
his sharp teeth.

Then
he went back.

**KNOCK!
KNOCK!
KNOCK!**

"Let me in,"
said the wolf.
"I am
your mother,
and I'm hungry!"

8

"Oh, no!"
cried the children.
"You are not
our mother.
We can see
your
wicked
eyes.
Go away!"

9

The wolf
went away,
and put on
dark glasses.

Then
he went back.

KNOCK!
KNOCK!
KNOCK!

"Let me in,"
said the wolf.
"I really am
your mother."

10

But
he couldn't be
their mother,
because
their mother
was already there.

"Oh, no!"
said the children.
"You couldn't be
our mother.
Besides,
we can still see
your
bushy
tail!"

The wolf
went away,
and shaved
his bushy tail.

As he went back,
everyone
laughed at him.

The wolf
was mad.

He was
so mad,
he ran
straight
at the door.

BUT –
this time,
the door
flew open.

"Come inside!"
cried the children.
"It's time
for dinner."

13

Poor
old
wolf!
He had no claws
to stop himself.
He had no teeth
to bite with.
He had no tail
to speak of
and
he could hardly see.

He went **ZIP!**

PLOP!

into the cooking pot.

And that night,
they had
Wolf Dinner.

And they had it
the next night

and

the next night

and

the next night . . .

until
they had all had
quite enough.

NO MORE
WOLF!

~Menu~

SUNDAY –
ROAST WOLF

MONDAY –
COLD WOLF
AND SALAD

TUESDAY –
CURRIED WOLF

WEDNESDAY
WOLF ON
TOAST

THURSDAY –
WOLFBURGERS
AND CHIPS

Little Brown Bird
finds a home

Little Brown Bird was ready
to lay some eggs.
But she had no home.
"Oh deary, deary me!"
said Little Brown Bird.
"Where can I find
a good home
for my eggs?"

She went to Dog.

"I'm ready
to lay my eggs,"
she said.
"But I have
no home.
Can we live
with you?"

"What a silly
you are!"
said Dog.
"I chase
little birds.
This is no home
for you.
You can take
some threads
from my blanket.
But
THAT IS ALL."

Little
Brown
Bird
flew off
and told
her husband.

Then she went to Horse.

"I'm ready
to lay my eggs,"
she said.
"But I have
no home.
Can we
live with you?"

"What a silly
you are!"
said Horse.
"I stamp at birds.
This is no home
for you.
You can take
some hay
from my box.
But
THAT IS ALL."

Little
Brown
Bird
flew off
and told her husband.

Then she went
to Cat
(but not too close).

"I'm ready
to lay my eggs,"
she said.
"But I have
no home.
Can we live
in your basket
when you're not
there?"

19

"What a silly
you are!"
said Cat.
"I *eat*
little birds.
This is no home
for you.
Take some fur
from my basket
IF YOU DARE."

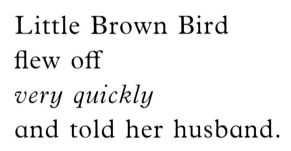

Little Brown Bird
flew off
very quickly
and told her husband.

She said,
"Dog won't
have us.
Horse won't
have us.
Cat will
eat us!
Oh, what shall
we do!"

"Ask Duck," said
her husband.

So Little Brown Bird
went to Duck.

"I'm ready
to lay my eggs,"
she said.
"But I have
no home.
Can we
live with you?"

21

"Of course!"
said Duck.
"You can live
in this nice mud
and swim with us."

"But we can't swim!"
said Little Brown Bird.

"Too bad!" said Duck.
"There is mud
and there is water
but
THAT IS ALL."

Little
Brown
Bird
flew off
and told
her husband.

"Perfect!" said
her husband.
"That is just
what we need."

Little
Brown
Bird
was very, very sad.

"I am ready
to lay
my eggs,"
she said.
"But I have
no home.
And I have
a crazy husband.
All we have
is mud, hay,
threads and fur.
What kind of home
is THAT!"

"Come and look!"
said her husband.

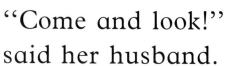

"Mud,

hay,

threads

and fur –

a perfect home
for little brown birds
like us."

And it was.

Would you like to sleep in a hole in the ground?

Would you like
to sleep
in a hole
in the ground?

Would you like
to sleep
in a tree?

Would you like
to snooze
in the ooze
of a pond –

or snore
in a bunch
like a bee?

Would you like
to sleep
on the wing
like a swift?

Would you like
to sleep
on the hoof?

Would you like
to hang
from your toes
all night –
upside-down
in the roof?

Would you like
to doze
in a dustbin?

Would you like
to curl up
in a cave?

Would you like
to dream
like a fish
in a stream –

or roll about
in a wave?

Would you like
to slumber
in rotten lumber
like a beaver
in a dam?

Or
are you happy
to jump into bed
at night,

snuggle up
tight,

turn out
the light

and imagine
whatever you like?

I AM!

Also available in the I CAN READ *series*

Giants and Princesses
Robbers and Witches